Napi and the fox

A traditional Blackfoot story as told by Ninaimsskaikkimaani

Illustrations by Marica Wierda

One day Napi and the fox were looking for food.
They walked for a long time but found nothing.
It was a nice warm day in fall.

They were very hungry.
As Napi went over a hill he saw four big buffalo.
They were resting in the grass.
Napi could not get close to them because the buffalo
would see him and run away.
Napi told the fox what he saw.

They tried to think of a plan to get to the buffalo. At last Napi said to the fox:

"My little brother, I have a plan. I will pluck all the fur off you, but will leave the fur at the tip of your tail. Then you go over the hill where the buffalo can see you. They will think you are so funny, they will laugh themselves to death."

The fox did not like the plan, but could not think of a better one.

He was so hungry that he agreed to do it.

Napi plucked all the hair from him but left the hair on the tip of his tail.

So the fox went over the top of the hill. He walked closer to the buffalo while doing all kind of tricks:

He walked on his front legs,
stood up on his hind legs,
jumped up into the air
and rolled over ...

When the buffalo first saw him they got up
on their feet.
They just looked at him; they did not know
what to think.

Then they began to laugh.
The more they looked at him the more they laughed.
They laughed till they were crying with laughter.

They laughed and laughed and
laughed, until they could laugh no more.
They laughed so much that one by one they fell down
and died.

Napi came over the hill and went down to the
buffalo.
He started to cut up the meat so he can carry it back
to his tipi.
By this time it had grown a little colder.
It was growing colder and colder.

Flakes of snow started falling down. Napi kept on talking to the fox that was sitting behind him.

"Ah, little brother," Napi said to the fox, "you did wonderful, I am not surprised that the buffalo laughed themselves to death. I nearly died myself as I watched you from the hill. You looked very funny".

The fox was very still with his mouth
open and his teeth shining. At last Napi had the
buffalo all skinned and the meat cut up.

Napi said to the fox: "It is getting pretty cold, isn't it?
Well, we do not care for the cold."

"We have all the meat we need to last us through winter. We will have nothing to do but feast and dance and sing until spring."
The fox did not reply.

Napi got angry and called out: "Why don't you answer me? Don't you hear me talking to you?"

Again the fox said nothing. Napi was mad and he
said: "Can't you speak?"
He walked up to the fox and gave him a push with
his foot.

The poor fox fell over. He was dead.
His body all covered in snow and ice.

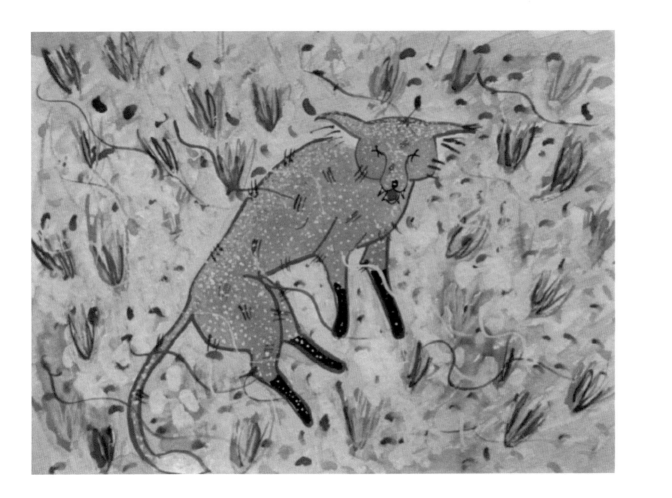

The Blackfoot used every part of the buffalo they hunted

The bones were used in making toys and playthings. For example the ribs were used as sled runners. Skulls were used in ceremonies and also as a tool for removing the hair from skin ropes. They made weapons, like shields and spear points from the skins and bones. The horns were special because they were used for spoons, cups, ladles and headdress ornaments.

Other uses were for riding and moving gear such as saddles and a variety of skin bags to carry things, such as berries, with. A variety of clothing was made from hides, both with and without hair; for example robes and moccasins. The hair was used as material to fill rawhide balls with. Tipi covers and bedding were also made from skins and the tails and hair were used to make tipi decorations from.

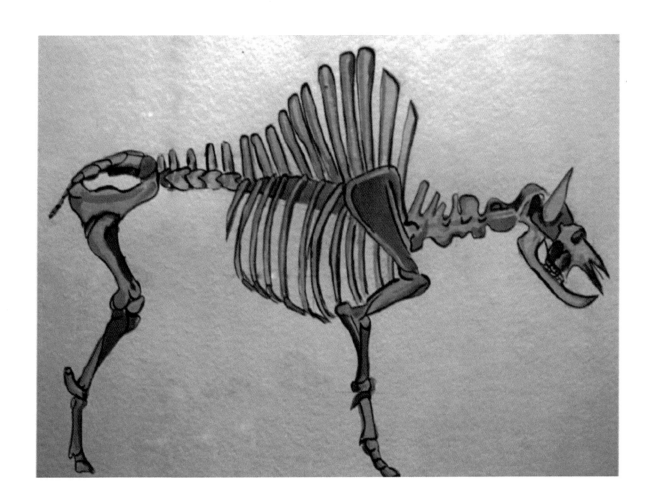

Further reading

- Gibson, Karen. B. **The Blackfeet: people of moccasins.** Bridgestone Books, 2003. ISBN: 0-7368-1565-1
- Grinnell, George. B. **Blackfoot lodge tales.** The New York Public Library, 2011. ISBN: 978-1-13105-480-3
- **Nitsitapiisinni: The story of the Blackfoot people.** Buffalo, N.Y.: Firefly Books, 2001. ISBN: 1-552297-583-5
- Rebus, Anna. **The Blackfoot.** Weigl Educational Publishers, 2009. ISBN: 978-1-55388-331-9

Manufactured by Amazon.ca
Bolton, ON

31807043R00021